4 ANNE WALLACE

A Valentine Fantasy

CAROLYN HAYWOOD

illustrated by Glenys and Victor Ambrus

William Morrow and Company
New York 1976

JP

5

Library of Congress Cataloging in Publication Data

Haywood, Carolyn (date)
  A valentine fantasy.

  SUMMARY: A tale of how Valentine's Day came into existence
and of how the heart became its symbol.
  [1. Fairy tales. 2. St. Valentine's Day—Fiction]
I. Ambrus, Glenys. II. Ambrus, Victor G. III. Title
PZ8.H339Val   [E]   75-23083
ISBN 0-688-22055-1
ISBN 0-688-32055-4 (lib. bdg.)

Awb

Dedicated by the author,
with warm affection,
to Rosemary Weber,
who listened patiently and encouragingly
to the unfoldment of this story.

The illustrators dedicate this book
with affection to the author,
Miss Carolyn Haywood.

Once there was a boy named Valentine.
At his birth, his uncle, a famous goldsmith,
gave Valentine a beautiful bow
and made a set of gold-tipped arrows for it.
Valentine was indeed a fortunate child.
As he grew up, he went
to live with his uncle and learn his art.
His uncle also taught him
how to use the bow and arrows,
and he became a fine marksman.

They set up a target
and practiced shooting at it over and over again.
Valentine, however, never shot
any of the birds or animals of the forest,
for they were his friends.
And, of all the creatures he saw around him,
the bluebirds were his special friends.
His uncle had told him
about the rarest of all birds, the golden bluebird,
believed to have a heart of gold,
and Valentine always hoped to find it.

One day, when Valentine was still a little boy,
he wandered deep into the forest.
Without realizing, he went farther than ever before,
and suddenly he saw before him a gold-flecked bluebird
that seemed to shimmer in the sunshine.
"It is the golden bluebird!" he breathed aloud.
Then, to his amazement,
the bird came to him and perched on his shoulder.
Valentine spoke lovingly to the bird,
and, to Valentine's greater surprise,
the bird replied in speech that Valentine understood.

Now a king reigned over the land
where Valentine lived,
but there was no queen.
In time, however, the king met
the beautiful princess of a nearby kingdom
and fell deeply in love with her.
He longed to make her his queen,
and soon he told her of his desire.

In reply, she said,
"You must bring me a token of your love."
"What do you wish as a token?" the king asked.

"I have been told that deep in the forest
there lives a very rare bluebird
called the golden bluebird
because it has a heart of gold.
Bring me the heart of this bluebird,
and I shall marry you."

The king went back to his kingdom perplexed,
for he had no idea
how he could get a bluebird's golden heart.

Still, he called in his wise man
and told him of his problem.
The wise man looked through all his books
and at last found the page
that described the golden bluebird.
It said, "The very rare golden bluebird has a heart of gold.
This golden heart can be obtained
only by the hunter with the golden arrows."

The wise man closed the book and said,
"We must find the hunter with the golden arrows."
"Exactly!" said the king. "And be quick about it.
I must have the golden heart."
The wise man called
all of the king's messengers together
and told them of the king's demand.
"You must find a hunter," said the wise man,
"who shoots with a set of golden arrows."
The messengers ran off in all directions.

One of them went into the forest,
and there he met Valentine,
carrying his beautiful bow and arrows.
"What good fortune," said the messenger.
"I see you have golden arrows.
The king wishes you to shoot the rare golden bluebird,
as his beloved will marry him
only when he gives her
the golden heart of such a bluebird."

"But I have never shot
the birds or animals of the forest,"
said Valentine.
"I can't shoot the bluebird."
"You must," said the messenger. "The king demands it."

"It would break my heart
to shoot any bird,"
said Valentine.

"Better your heart broken
than the king's," said the messenger.
"Take me to the golden bluebird."
Valentine's heart was heavy
as he led the way deeper into the forest.
He hoped that his friend,
the golden bluebird, would not appear,
but late in the day he saw it fly into a tree.
"There it is!" cried the messenger.
"Quick, shoot it, so that I may get the heart."
"I will not shoot the bluebird," said Valentine.
"Not even for the king."
"Then I must take you to the palace dungeon,"
replied the king's messenger.
Valentine was dragged off to the dungeon.
On the way he lost his bow and arrows.

The dungeon was dark and cold; there was no bed.
Valentine had to sleep on a pile of straw
with no pillow for his head.

During the night Valentine was very restless.
Once he thought he heard the fluttering of wings.
"Surely," said Valentine to himself,
"there are no birds in this place."
Then, through his troubled sleep,
he heard someone calling, "Valentine! Valentine!"
He opened his eyes,
and again he heard the flutter of wings.
"Who's there?" Valentine asked.
A tiny voice replied, "Your friend, the bluebird.
I've come to save you."
"No one can save me," said Valentine.
"The king is angry with me,
because I would not shoot you for your golden heart.
Now I have lost my bow, my arrows, and my happiness."
"You saved my life," said the bluebird,
"and I shall save yours.
You have not lost your happiness,
for I have brought you a golden heart."
Valentine was astonished. He sat up.

"Oh, bluebird!" he cried.

"How can you have brought me a golden heart!
Surely your heart is still untouched and safe!"

"It is not my heart," said the bluebird,

"but it is exactly the same. Look, it is very beautiful."

The bird lowered his head,

and a chain on which a golden heart hung

slipped from his neck and fell into Valentine's hands.

"It is indeed beautiful!" said Valentine.

"How can I ever thank you?"

"And here is your bow and the rest of the arrows,"
said the bluebird.

He dropped them from his claws

to the floor beside Valentine.

"I found your bow and arrows near the castle,

and I knew you were in trouble," said the bluebird.

"So I flew to your uncle, the goldsmith,

and from one of the arrows

he fashioned a heart for you."

"Oh, how happy I am," cried Valentine.

"Now the king will surely be satisfied."

When the keeper of the dungeon appeared,
Valentine showed him the golden heart.
Immediately the doors were opened,
and Valentine was set free.
He hurried to the king's chambers
and gave the heart to the wise man,
who gave it to the king and told him of Valentine.

"It is very beautiful," said the king,
"but I hope the princess will not be disappointed
when she learns that it is not
really the heart of the bluebird."
"Let us find out, Your Majesty," said the wise man.
"I think that the princess
will be delighted with this golden heart."

So the king called for his fastest horse.
Carrying the golden heart in a red velvet box,
he rode off at great speed.

The sky was brilliant with the setting sun
when the king reached the palace
where the princess lived.

He found her sitting in the garden feeding the birds,
and he fell upon his knee.
Holding out his gift, he said,
"My beloved, here is my token."
The princess took the box and opened it.
When she saw the golden heart,
she cried, "How beautiful!
Is it really the heart of the golden bluebird?"
"No, my love," said the king,
"but it is fashioned like the golden bluebird's heart.
I hope it pleases you."
"It does, indeed," the princess replied.
"I have been watching the birds feeding.
Among them was a beautiful bluebird,
and it saddened me to think
that I had asked you to bring me
the heart of the golden bluebird.
I wept for shame, but now my happiness has returned,
and I shall be your queen."

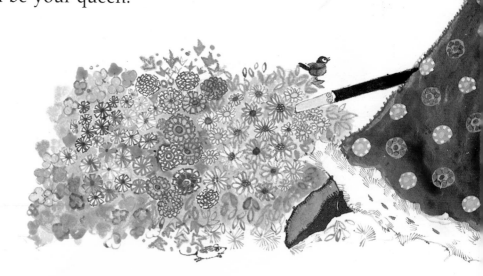

Overjoyed, the king told the princess
the story of Valentine.
"This is a very important day!" said the princess.
"We should remember it in some special way."
The king held up his hand. "It shall be so," he said.
"From now on, the fourteenth of February
shall be known as Valentine's Day.
All lovers shall give a heart,
fashioned in any manner, to their beloved,
and it shall be called a valentine."
When Valentine heard of the king's announcement,

he was deeply moved,
for now his name would bring happiness to many.
He came as an honored guest to the king's wedding,
and flocks of bluebirds,
with the golden bluebird at their head,
appeared to circle around
the king and his beautiful queen.
And so it is that, on the fourteenth day of February,
lovers declare themselves
with valentines adorned with hearts.
In this way, they say, "I love you."

About the Author

Carolyn Haywood was born in Philadelphia
and now lives in Chestnut Hill, a suburb of that city.
A graduate of the Philadelphia Normal School,
she also studied at the Pennsylvania Academy of Fine Arts,
where she won the Cresson European Scholarship.
Her first story, *"B" Is for Betsy*, was published in 1939.
Since then she has written books almost every year
and has become one of the most widely read American writers
for younger children.

About the Artists

Victor Ambrus was born in Budapest, Hungary,
and Glenys Ambrus in London, England.
Both are graduates of the Royal College of Art, in London,
and are noted illustrators.
Mr. Ambrus won the 1965 Kate Greenaway Medal in England
for his picture book *The Three Poor Tailors*,
and he has illustrated many books for older children as well.
At present, Mr. and Mrs. Ambrus and their two sons
live in Farnham, Surrey, England.